THE FOUR MUSICIANS

Illustrated by Wendy Edelson

Adapted by Mary Rowitz

Louis Weber, C.E.O.
Publications International, Ltd.
7373 North Cicero Avenue
Lincolnwood, Illinois 60712

www.pilbooks.com

Manufactured in China.

8 7 6 5 4 3 2 1

ISBN: 0-7853-7879-0

One day a donkey was walking by the barn. He stopped when he heard his owner talking with another farmer. "I know what you mean," the one farmer said. "Sometimes it's easier to just get a younger one."

The donkey wondered what they could be talking about. His owner continued, "He is old and cannot pull the plow anymore. It's time to put that old donkey out to pasture."

The donkey couldn't believe his ears! They were talking about him! He was very hurt to hear these words. "Hee-haw!" said the donkey. "I won't be sent out to pasture. I'll go to the town of Bremen and become a musician."

The donkey had just started on his way when he saw a sad dog sitting by the road. "My owner says I am too old to hunt," howled the dog. "He wants to get a younger dog who keeps quiet."

"Come with me to Bremen and we will work as musicians," said the donkey. "We'll be a team."

"Woof!" said the dog. "I really like that idea!" The two hadn't gone far before they crossed paths with a gloomy cat. They asked what was wrong.

"My owner says I am too old to catch mice," he cried. "She is going to get a younger cat."

They invited the cat to come to Bremen and sing with them. "Mee-ow!" answered the cat, and the three were on their way.

The dog, cat, and donkey were walking when a very upset rooster flew into the middle of the road. "Cock-a-doodle-day!" the rooster squawked.

"What a strong voice you have!" the dog said.

"My owners say there is no point in having a strong voice if you don't use it every day," crowed the rooster. "They plan to serve me for dinner!"

"Join us on our trip," said the dog. "We are going to work as musicians. We could use your strong voice to make our band complete."

"Cock-a-doodle-day!" said the rooster. "Let's be on our way!" The four new friends practiced singing as they walked toward Bremen.

Nighttime came. Just when the four musicians found a nice tree to camp under, the rooster saw something. "I think I see a light shining from inside a house!" he said. "It doesn't seem far away."

"They might have some food to share," said the dog. "A big, juicy bone sounds mighty good right about now."

"Mmmm, a bowl of milk would be purr-fect," purred the cat.

"A plate of corn certainly would hit the spot," crowed the rooster. The donkey thought it all sounded good. The four set out for the house.

They walked up to the house. The donkey, being the tallest of the group, peered inside the window. "What do you see?" asked the cat.

"There are four men sitting at a table that is covered with food," the donkey said. "They must eat like kings every night. There are stacks of gold everywhere."

"What do we do now?" asked the rooster. "Do we just knock on the door and ask for food?"

The donkey shook his head. "Remember we are going to be musicians," he said. "We should practice singing for our supper." They thought this was a grand idea. Very carefully, they planned their first concert.

The four musicians decided to stand one on top of the other so everyone could be heard. First the donkey took his place near the bottom of the window. Then the dog jumped on his back. The cat made his way up to the dog's back. Finally the rooster flew up to the top.

They all faced the window and cleared their throats. When the donkey gave the signal, they began to sing.

Never has there been a louder or mightier group effort! The four friends tried to sing better than they ever had before. What they didn't know is that it didn't sound like singing. It sounded like "Hee-haw! Woof! Mee-ow! Cock-a-doodle-day!"

The four friends also did not know that the men were really robbers. They were hiding out and counting gold they had stolen. When they heard the all the loud noise, they looked out the window. They saw what looked like a four-headed beast. "Run! Run! Run!" one robber yelled. "Run before the four-headed beast gets us!"

The animals were confused. Why had the men run away? The donkey said, "They must be going to get more people to hear our concert."

"I say we go inside and have some dinner as a reward for our splendid singing," the rooster said.

"Indeed!" agreed the donkey. "That is a grand idea!" The four musicians went into the house.

They were so hungry that they ate every last bite! Soon after the meal, they were very sleepy. Since they were already inside the house, they agreed it would be best to spend the night there. Besides, they didn't want to miss the people who were going to come hear them perform.

The donkey lay in the middle of the room. The dog stretched out near the door. The cat curled up near the fireplace, and the rooster flew up to a beam near the ceiling.

It didn't take long for their tired eyes to close. They were all quite sound asleep when the door knob slowly began to turn. They were still asleep when someone tiptoed into the room.

One robber had come back. He thought he saw a glow from the coals in the fireplace. It was really the cat's eyes. When he lit a match to start a fire, the cat jumped up. The robber tripped over the dog. The dog bit his leg, causing the robber to stumble over the donkey. The donkey kicked the robber. The rooster woke up and began crowing, "Cock-a-doodle-day! Leave without delay!"

The robber ran as fast as his legs would carry him. He told the others to stay away forever or the four-headed beast would get them.

The four musicians lived in the house for the rest of their days. They were quite happy giving free concerts and using the gold to buy food.